Goddess Girls

ATHENA
THE
BRAIN

READ THE OTHER BOOKS IN THE

GODDESS GIRLS SERIES

Persephone the Phony

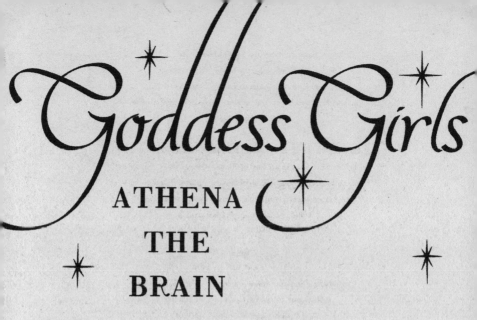

Goddess Girls

ATHENA
THE
BRAIN

JOAN HOLUB & SUZANNE WILLIAMS

Aladdin

NEW YORK   LONDON   TORONTO   SYDNEY

ALADDIN

An imprint of Simon & Schuster Children's Publishing Division

1230 Avenue of the Americas, New York, NY 10020

First Aladdin paperback edition April 2010

Text copyright © 2010 by Joan Holub & Suzanne Williams

All rights reserved, including the right of reproduction
in whole or in part in any form.

ALADDIN is a trademark of Simon & Schuster, Inc., and related logo
is a registered trademark of Simon & Schuster, Inc.

For information about special discounts for bulk purchases,
please contact Simon & Schuster Special Sales at 1-866-506-1949
or business@simonandschuster.com.

The Simon & Schuster Speakers Bureau can bring authors to your live event.
For more information or to book an event contact the Simon & Schuster Speakers
Bureau at 1-866-248-3049 or visit our website at www.simonspeakers.com.

Designed by Karin Paprocki

The text of this book was set in Baskerville Handcut Regular.

Manufactured in the United States of America

0611 OFF

8 10 9 7

Library of Congress Control Number 2009019170

ISBN 978-1-4169-8271-5

ISBN 978-1-4169-9912-6 (eBook)

For Paula McMillin, Sherylee Vermaak,

and goddessgirls everywhere

–J. H. and S. W.

CONTENTS

1

The Letter

A STRANGE, GLITTERY BREEZE WHOOSHED into Athena's bedroom window one morning, bringing a rolled-up piece of papyrus with it. She jumped up from her desk and watched in amazement as it swirled above her.

"A message for Athena from Mount Olympus!" the wind howled. "Art thou present?"

"Yes, I'm thou. I'm present. I mean—I'm Athena," she replied in a rush.

Abruptly the breeze stilled, and the scroll dropped right in the middle of her science homework. A thrill swept over her. She'd never gotten a message from the gods before! No human she knew ever had. The gods and goddesses on Mount Olympus ruled Earth, but only made their powers known for important matters. What could they want? Was she being given an urgent mission to save the world?

She unrolled the scroll as fast as she could and began to read.

DEAR ATHENA,

THIS MAY COME AS A SHOCK TO YOU,

BUT I, ZEUS—KING OF THE GODS

AND RULER OF THE HEAVENS—AM

YOUR FATHER. AND THAT, OF COURSE,

MAKES YOU A GODDESS.

"Huh?" Athena's knees wobbled so hard that she

plopped back into her chair. She read on:

YOU MUST BE, WHAT . . . NINE YEARS

OLD NOW?

"Try twelve," she mumbled under her breath. And

for most of those years, she had yearned to know who

her parents were. She'd spun endless stories in her

head, imagining how they looked and what they were

like.

At last a piece of the puzzle had dropped into her

lap. Or onto her desk, anyway. Her eyes raced across the rest of the letter as she continued:

AT ANY RATE, YOU'RE PLENTY OLD

ENOUGH NOW TO CONTINUE YOUR

SCHOOLING AT MOUNT OLYMPUS

ACADEMY, WHERE I—YOUR DEAR

OL' DAD—AM THE PRINCIPAL. I HEREBY

COMMAND YOU TO PREPARE AT

ONCE FOR THE JOURNEY TO MOUNT

OLYMPUS. HERMES DELIVERY SERVICE

WILL PICK YOU UP TOMORROW MORNING.

YOURS IN THUNDER,

ZEUS

* * *

Was this for real? She could hardly believe it! Beneath his signature was the worst drawing she'd ever seen. It looked sort of like a caterpillar, but Athena had a feeling it was supposed to be a muscled arm. She grinned. One thing was for sure, Zeus was no artist.

A blazing gold *Z* shaped like a thunderbolt—Zeus's official seal—was embossed alongside the drawing. She traced her finger over it.

"Ow!" A burst of electricity buzzed her fingertip, and she dropped the scroll. As the sizzle zinged through her, the scroll shut with a snap and rolled across the carpet. No question about it, this letter was from the King of Mount Olympus!

Feeling dazed—and *not* from the electricity—she gulped. She was his *daughter.* A goddess!

Athena jumped to her feet, unsure if she should be happy or upset, but feeling a little of both. Rushing over to the mirror, she gazed at her reflection. Her determined gray eyes stared back at her, looking no different from before she'd read the letter. And her long, wavy brown hair was the same too. With a poke of one finger, she squished the end of her too-long nose up, then frowned at the piggy nose she'd made.

She wasn't sure what she'd expected to see in the glass. To suddenly look beautiful, wise, and powerful? In other words—more like a goddess?

She turned as she heard her best friend Pallas come into their bedroom.

Crunch! Crunch!

Pallas eyed her, munching an apple. "What's that?" she asked, gesturing toward the letter on the floor.

"Umm." Athena quickly scooped it up and tucked it behind her back.

Looking suspicious, Pallas came closer, trying to see what it was. "Come on. Give. I've known you forever. Why are you suddenly keeping secrets?"

Athena thumped one end of the scroll gently against her back. On one hand, she wanted to twirl around and shout the news that she was a goddess! At the same time she wanted to hide the letter in the back of her closet and pretend it hadn't come.

Zeus's summons was going to change *everything*.

"It's a letter," she finally admitted. "From my dad. Turns out he's . . . Zeus."

Pallas stopped in mid-munch, her mouth full of apple. "Wha? Zeu?" Quickly she finished chewing and swallowed. "Your dad is the King of the Gods?"

Athena nodded, holding out the papyrus scroll.

Pallas pounced on it. By the time she finished reading, her eyes were huge. "You're a *goddess*?" Her voice rose to a squeak on the last word.

"I don't want this to change things," Athena said quickly. "We'll still be best friends, right?"

Pallas examined the scroll closely, seeming not to hear. "Who brought it?"

"The wind."

"It's got the official seal and everything. It's the real thing, then—an invitation to Mount Olympus." Pallas stared at Athena in wonderment. "My best friend is a goddess!"

"So you think I should go?" Even as Athena asked, she knew that the idea of going to Mount Olympus Academy was growing on her. But how could she tell Pallas that? She'd be devastated at the thought of Athena moving away.

Pallas tossed the scroll on her bed. It rolled itself tight and snapped shut again. "Are you crazy? Of course you have to go!" she exclaimed. "This is your chance to really be somebody! I mean, who *wouldn't* want to be a goddess?"

Athena hugged herself and glanced out the window toward the Triton River, feeling a little hurt. It almost sounded like Pallas was trying to get rid of her. She'd lived with Pallas's family since she was a baby. The two of them had shared this room and been as close as sisters all their lives.

"But I'll miss you, Pal," Athena said softly.

Pallas came to the window and looped her arm through one of Athena's. Her voice was softer now, as if she'd just realized she'd be losing her best friend. "Yeah. I'll miss you, too." She took a deep breath. "But you've always wondered about your parents. This is your chance to find out about them. Besides, it doesn't sound like Zeus is giving you much choice."

Athena nodded. "His letter *is* kind of bossy." She stuck her nose in the air haughtily as she quoted him in a deep, authoritative voice. "I hereby command you to prepare at once for the journey to Mount Olympus."

Pallas giggled. "Yours in thunder . . . ," she mimicked in a loud, bass tone.

"Zeus!" they finished together. They fell on their beds in a fit of laughter.

"I guess going against a god's wishes—even if he *is* my dad—might be a bad idea," said Athena once she'd calmed down. "If he got mad, he might just bean me on the head with one of his thunderbolts."

Pallas's face went pale, and she rose on one elbow to gaze over at her. "You don't suppose he's *violent?*"

"Don't worry," Athena said quickly, turning on her side toward Pallas. "I'm sure we'll get along just fine." But she couldn't help remembering that thunderbolt and feeling a little nervous about meeting her powerful dad.

She reached out to a toy on her bedside table—a wooden horse named Woody. "I wonder what the academy will be like," she mused as she idly finger-combed the rope mane on the back of her favorite childhood toy.

"I bet the godboys and goddessgirls who go there are all brainy like you." Pallas propped her head up on one fist. "In fact, I can hardly believe we didn't guess you might be a goddess. I mean, you learned to knit *and* do math when you were only three years old! You're way smarter than the rest of us."

Athena shrugged, knowing it was true. Her studies here on Earth were so easy they were boring.

"And there's the other stuff too," Pallas hinted softly.

Athena winced, looking away. *Weird* stuff, Pallas meant, though she was too nice to say it. Like the day Athena had invented the very first flute and trumpet ever seen on Earth, and then played an impromptu concert, even though she knew nothing about music.

And then there was the time she'd been reading about owls and thinking how fun it would be to fly. Suddenly her feet had left the ground and her hair had turned into bristly brown feathers. Right in the middle of gym class, too! Luckily, she had changed back almost immediately, and everyone had assumed she'd been affected by some random bit of magic in the air, which might have floated down from Mount Olympus that day.

From then on, she'd been more careful about who was around when she did things like that. But some of the kids still nicknamed her "birdbrain" as a result of the episode.

"I'm tired of trying to hide that I'm different. It would be nice to fit in for a change," Athena admitted. "I only wish you could come too."

Pallas shook her head. "I don't belong where you're going. But hey! Maybe I can visit you. If it's not against the rules, I mean."

Athena brightened. "Yeah! I'll ask Zeus when I get there."

Pallas sat up. "So you're definitely going?"

A slow smile spread across Athena's face, and she nodded, sitting up on her knees. "Like you said, who *wouldn't* want to be a goddess?"

Pallas hopped up from her bed and grinned at her friend. "C'mon, let's go tell my parents and then I'll help you pack."

While Pallas's mom and dad checked out that Zeus's letter was for real, Athena began packing. The two girls spent the rest of the day scurrying around, as Athena prepared to leave the only home she'd ever known.

"An entire suitcase full of scrolls?" Pallas teased at one point. "Don't you think they'll have a library at the academy?"

"I'm not taking any chances," said Athena. Carefully she stuffed the suitcase full of textscrolls written by her favorite Greek authors, including Plato, Aristotle, and Aesop. Then she added her own notescrolls, which contained her invention and knitting ideas, and ideas for science and math projects.

By that evening, she'd packed her entire life into two suitcases and one bag. She was exhausted—mentally and physically—but she and Pallas stayed up half the night anyway, talking and giggling about what Zeus and the other gods might be like.

"I wonder which godboys and goddessgirls go to the academy?" Athena mused excitedly. "I wonder if I'll meet any Amazons. I wonder if I'll get to ride Pegasus."

"Promise me you'll let me know if you get to meet any cool godboys like Poseidon," said Pallas. "I'm dying to know if he's as cute as the sculpture of him we saw in Crete last summer."

"It'll be my first priority," Athena teased.

"I hope he's not stuck-up."

"Me too," said Athena. "I hope none of the godboys and goddessgirls are."

Pallas grinned dreamily. "I can hardly wait to tell everyone at school tomorrow that you're a goddess!" She yawned. "Well, night-night, Athena. Let's get up early, and I'll make owl-face pancakes for breakfast before you go. The kind with ears and blueberry eyes that you liked when we were little." Her voice drifted away.

After Pallas dozed off, Athena tossed and turned until sunrise, dreaming of Mount Olympus. In some of her dreams, she was the star of the academy, getting the highest academic honors. In other dreams—night-mares, really—Zeus hurled thunderbolts at her for embarrassing him with failing grades.

Before she knew it, morning arrived and she was hugging Pallas's parents good-bye as they left for work. Just as she and Pallas were finishing the pancakes they'd made for breakfast, there was a knock on the door. Hermes had come, wearing winged sandals, a winged cap, and a knee-length toga. Beyond him on the lawn sat a beautiful silver chariot that was already piled high with packages.

"Where are you supposed to sit?" Pallas whispered from behind her.

"Good question," Athena whispered back. And it was curious that there weren't any horses attached to the chariot.

"Hup! Hup! We're behind schedule." Hermes pushed some packages around to make room for her. Then he rushed Athena, her bag, and her two suitcases aboard as if she were just another package he needed to deliver. And in a way, she guessed she was.

The minute she settled in, mighty white wings sprouted from the chariot's sides. "Strap yourself in!" ordered Hermes, as the wings began to flap. Athena fastened the strap and twisted around as the chariot lifted off.

"Bye! I'll miss you, Pal!" she called over her shoulder.

"I'll miss you, too!" Pallas shouted, waving. "Don't forget to ask Zeus about a visit!"

"Okay!" Athena called back.

Two girls from their mathematics class joined Pallas just then, on their way to Triton Junior High. Pallas pointed at the chariot, talking excitedly, probably telling them the whole story of Zeus's letter, Athena guessed.

"Promise you won't forget me!" Athena shouted.

"What?" Pallas shouted back, cupping her ear as she tried to hear. As Hermes flew higher into the sky, the chariot's shadow fell across a sea of glistening white clouds.

"I said, don't forget me!" Athena tried again. But Pallas only shook her head, looking confused. Still, Athena kept waving until the three girls were only specks walking to school together alongside the Triton River below.

Of course Pallas would make new friends once she was gone, Athena knew. But that thought didn't comfort her a bit. She didn't want Pallas to find a new best friend! Sadness washed over her at the thought, and a tear trickled down her cheek. She wiped it away. She couldn't show up at her new school with puffy eyes.

Suddenly the chariot lurched. Then it began to wobble and bounce. The wings at its sides flapped wildly as it seemed to lose its balance.

Athena jerked around in her seat, her eyes wide. "What's going on?"

The muscles in Hermes' arms bulged as he struggled with the stick shift to steady the wings. Grumbling, he thumped the dials on the instrument panel with the side of his fist.

The corners of jostling packages poked Athena's arms and legs as she held on for dear life. "What's wrong?" she demanded.

"We're overweight. Got to offload some ballast." Hermes eyed her, and for a second she worried he was going to toss *her* out. Instead he lobbed both of her suitcases over the side of the chariot.

"Wait! My notescrolls!" she protested. Heartbroken, she could only watch them fall. Her invention ideas! Her journals! All her thoughts and ideas from the past twelve years had been written on those scrolls. Now they were gone, along with most of her textscrolls. All she was left with was a single bag, which contained some of her clothes, a bundle of knitting, and a biography about Pythagoras she'd been reading.

"You could have at least asked which bag I wanted to keep!" she protested. Hermes didn't answer. By now the wind was whooshing past so loudly she wasn't even sure he'd heard.

As they traveled on, Athena caught glimpses of green fields, blue seas, and cityscapes below. But they faded away as the winged chariot flew ever higher.

Soon they began circling the top of a gigantic mountain. "Next stop: Mount Olympus Academy," rumbled Hermes. Athena leaned forward trying to see it, her long hair whipping in the wind behind her.

With a burst of speed the chariot broke through a fluffy cloud. Up ahead, her new school sprang into view almost like magic. The majestic academy gleamed in the sunlight atop the highest mountain in Greece. Built of polished white stone, it was five stories tall and surrounded on all sides by dozens of Ionic columns. Low-relief friezes were sculpted just below its peaked rooftop.

Looks like I've traded Pallas for a palace, thought Athena.

Below in the courtyard, dozens of students were rushing around. Everyone seemed to have someplace to go. These were godboys and goddessgirls, she realized. How strange to think that she was one of them. Were they nice? Would they like her? Athena clutched her bag tight.

"Too late to change your mind now," said Hermes. How had he guessed she was having second thoughts? He touched down at the top of the granite steps leading up to the school and scooted her out of the chariot. Then, without another word, he took off in a rush, leaving her behind with her bag. Probably had another urgent package to deliver.

He'd left her standing in front of a huge white door. Letters chiseled on it read THE OFFICE. A water fountain stood just outside. Parched from her journey, Athena bent to take a gulp from it and quickly discovered that, instead of water, it spouted some kind of juice she'd never tasted before. It was so delicious that she took a second drink.

When she straightened again, she noticed her hand looked kind of weird—like it had been powdered with golden glitter. Tilting it side to side, she saw that it sparkled in the sunlight. So did her arm. So did *both* of her arms! And her legs, too.

Her skin had begun to shimmer—just like a real goddess!

2
First Day

THE NINE-HEADED LADY BEHIND THE COUN-
ter in the front office stared at Athena with all eighteen
of her eyes. "You must be the new student Zeus told
me to expect."

Startled, Athena tried to decide which head to reply
to. The grumpy green one, the icky orange one, the
impatient purple one, or . . . ? Before she could answer,

the heads all spoke at the same time again. "Athena, correct? From Earth?"

Athena nodded. Finding her tongue at last, she said, "I'm here to register for classes."

"Ms. Hydra?" A noisy group of students had come in with questions. All but one of the lady's heads turned away to answer.

"Right, then," the orange head continued to Athena. "You'll find your class choices, your locker combination, and your dorm room assignment in this packet." Ms. Hydra shoved it across the counter to her. "Classes are in the main building, floors one through three. Dorms are upstairs—girls on floor four and boys on five. Any questions?"

"Um . . ." Athena's head was spinning just trying to remember everything. She pulled out the class list.

What had happened to philosophy, rhetoric, and mathematics? she wondered. Instead she saw a list of classes she'd never heard of back at Triton Junior High. She checked off five of the choices: Hero-ology, Spell-ology, Revenge-ology, Beast-ology, and Beautyology. She wanted to learn as much as she could, as fast as possible.

Ms. Hydra looked a little concerned as she handed over five textscrolls—a different-colored one for each class. "*Five* classes? That's quite a load for your first semester here. Are you sure?"

The woman obviously had no idea who she was dealing with. Everyone back in Triton knew Athena was a brain. Still, if she'd had time for second thoughts, she might've dropped a class. But a lyrebell sounded in the hall behind her, and she was worried she'd be late.

"Sure, I'm sure." Juggling everything she'd been given, she headed out of the office.

"Wait! Don't forget this." Ms. Hydra tossed her one last scroll. It was pale pink and tied with a sparkly silver ribbon. The words *Goddessgirl Guide* were written on the outside of it in swirly pink letters.

"Thanks," Athena called. The sundial outside the window in the courtyard showed she had only ten minutes to find her locker and get to her first class. As she hurried off, she turned her head this way and that, taking note of everything so she could tell Pallas about it when she wrote her later.

The academy was so beautiful! There were gleaming marble floor tiles and golden fountains. And the domed ceiling was covered with paintings illustrating the glorious exploits of the gods and goddesses.

One showed Zeus battling giants who were storming Mount Olympus carrying torches and spears. Another showed him driving a chariot pulled by four white horses across the sky while hurling thunderbolts into the clouds. That was *her* dad up there! Suddenly Athena felt a pang of sadness. Pallas would have loved this! If only she were here to see everything too.

Other students rushed past Athena to class. She stared after one with a scaly tail and horns, goggled at a slimy one with webbed feet, and rubbed her eyes in disbelief at another that was part horse.

Three girls in particular caught her attention. Even among other amazing immortals, these girls stood out. One was extraordinarily beautiful, with long, shimmery golden hair. Another, whose hair was short and black, strode along confidently with a quiver of arrows slung across her back and a bow hanging over her shoulder. The third was delicate and pale, with curly red hair. All three had graceful figures and wore flowing gowns called chitons, a fashion that was all the rage in Greece now. And their skin shimmered lightly, just like hers.

Heads turned to follow them as they walked down the hall. As Athena gaped too, she saw that identical gold necklaces with dangling double G-shaped charms hung from the necks of all three girls. "Hey, goddess-girls!" someone called to them, waving. So that was what the double *G*s stood for.

At the top of the stairs, Athena noticed three more girls, each with skin the color of spring leaves, and long green hair that was so dark it almost looked black. She glanced at their faces and gave a start. They were triplets! Except for one thing: Only two had skin that shimmered.

As she stared at them, she realized they were staring back.

"Hi," she said, smiling. But the trio looked away. She tried not to let her feelings be hurt. These girls might be standoffish, but that didn't mean everyone else would be too. After all, she couldn't expect to make tons of friends her very first day.

Suddenly a boy in front of her sprouted giant wings, startling her into dropping several of her scrolls. A passing teacher grabbed him by his pointed ear. "No shape-shifting in the halls. You've just earned yourself a demerit, godboy."

Athena knelt to pick up her stuff. Everything was so different here from back home. It was fascinating, but also a little scary. In Triton she'd tried so hard to be like the other kids, but she'd somehow always felt apart from them. Maybe she could be herself here, where everyone was a bit weird.

"Hey, are you new?" asked a voice. "Where are you from?"

Standing, Athena stared in surprise at the girl who'd spoken. Her hair was streaked blue and gold, and her bangs were plastered against her forehead in the shape of a question mark. Her skin didn't shimmer. Was she a mortal? Would it be rude to ask?

"What's your name?" the girl asked, despite the fact that Athena hadn't yet replied to her first two questions. Continuing down the hall with her, the stranger talked a mile a minute. She seemed to ask any question that came into her head.

Spying her locker, Athena stopped and opened it. When the girl paused for a breath, Athena blurted, "I'm Athena. What's your—?"

But before she could finish, the girl fired more questions: "Athena, huh? So when did you get here? This morning? What classes are you taking?"

Athena gave up trying to get a word in and shoved as much stuff as she could into her locker.

"So, who've you got first period?" the girl went on. "Is it—?"

"Hi, Pandora," said a new voice.

Athena turned. It was one of the three beautiful goddessgirls she'd noticed earlier the golden-haired one wearing a double G-charm necklace. Her long, glossy tresses were threaded with ribbons and held back from her face with shell-shaped clips that matched both her sparkling blue eyes and the belt she wore at the waist of her white chiton. Up close, she was a breathtaking beauty unlike any Athena had ever seen—even in *Teen Scrollazine*.

"What's up, Aphrodite?" Pandora asked, grinning at her. "Wow! Where'd you get that great belt?"

Before the glamorous goddessgirl could even attempt a reply, Pandora turned away to stare at a godboy walking past.

Squish, squish, squish. His feet made squelching sounds, and he left wet footprints behind him with every step. He was holding a dripping three-pronged spear. With pale turquoise skin and eyes, he was the handsomest godboy Athena had seen so far. And he looked just like the statue she and Pallas had seen in Crete. The one of—

"Poseidon! Hey, where'd you get the cool pitchfork?" Pandora hollered, following him.

"It's called a *trident*," he informed her.

Athena stared after them. "Is Pandora a mortal?"

"Are you new?" asked Aphrodite at the same time.

They both laughed.

"I guess Pandora's curiosity is catching," said Aphrodite. She shifted the scrolls she was carrying from one hip to the other. "I'll go first. Yes, Pandora's a mortal. You can tell because her skin doesn't shimmer like ours. Okay, your turn."

Athena smiled at her. Aphrodite wasn't just beautiful, she was also nice. "I'm Athena. And yes, I'm new. I asked about Pandora because I wondered if mortals are allowed to go to school here. I have a friend back home on Earth who's mortal, and I thought maybe she could—"

Aphrodite shook her head, probably guessing what she'd been about to ask. "Pandora isn't just any mortal—the gods took great care when they created her, giving her special gifts."

"Curiosity?" guessed Athena.

"That and other things," said Aphrodite.

"But do other mortals go here? I saw three girls earlier," said Athena. "Triplets with green skin. One of them had skin that didn't shimmer."

Aphrodite nodded. "Medusa. Her two sisters are goddesses, but she's not. Only a few special mortals invited by Zeus are lucky enough to attend the academy with us. New students—mortal and immortal—come and go every semester at his whim. You must be something special to have been invited."

Special? She hoped she was, because it sounded like Zeus might decide to send her home if she didn't measure up, Athena realized with alarm. Imagine, her own father dismissing her from Mount Olympus Academy. That would be so embarrassing—not to mention an awful letdown.

Just then a herald appeared on a balcony at the end of the hall. "The first class of the academic year is now in session!" he announced in a loud, important voice. He hit a lyrebell with a little hammer.

Ping! Ping! Ping!

"Oh, no, we're late!" exclaimed Athena. She grabbed the textscroll for her first class and poked it into her bag. Hoisting its strap over her shoulder, she slammed her locker shut.

"No worries." Aphrodite said calmly. "The teachers always cut us some slack the first day. So where are you headed?"

"Hero-ology in room 208," said Athena. She had already memorized her class schedule and the corresponding room numbers.

Aphrodite smiled, which made her even more dazzling. "Me too. C'mon."

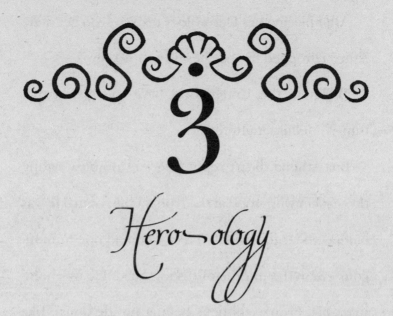

3

Hero-ology

INSIDE THE CLASSROOM THERE WERE ONLY two empty seats left, across the aisle from each other. Aphrodite and Athena took them. The girl directly behind Athena was one of the green-haired triplets she'd seen that morning outside the school. The one who didn't shimmer—Medusa. She was painting her fingernails green too, in her lap so the teacher couldn't see.

After placing her Hero-ology textscroll on her desk, Athena dropped her bag beside it with a clunk.

"What in the Underworld have you got in that thing?" Medusa muttered.

But Athena didn't reply. She was too busy ogling the teacher who stood at the front of the room. He was bald, with large, sandaled feet, and had one humongous eye in the middle of his forehead. He was holding a big, bronze soldier's helmet upside down, like a bowl.

"Good morning, class," he began. "I'm Mr. Cyclops, and this is Beginning Hero-ology."

He shook the helmet, and it made a clanking sound. Then he tilted it and showed them that it was filled with little painted statues. Each one was a person about three inches tall, with a card tied around its neck by a string.

"I've placed figures of your heroes inside this helmet," Mr. Cyclops said. "Without looking, please choose one and pass the helmet to the person behind you. Over the course of the semester, it'll be your job to guide the hero you've selected on a quest."

"I'll start with you, Dionysus." He handed the helmet to a boy with little horns on top of his head. He was seated at the head of the first row of desks. After taking a figure, the boy passed it to Poseidon, who was sitting behind him.

"If we don't like who we get, can we trade?" Medusa asked.

Mr. Cyclops's big eyeball squinted at her, and his single eyebrow bunched in irritation. "No trading."

"Now," he said, speaking to the class again. "You'll be scored on three skills in my class: manipulation, disasters, and quick saves. Any more questions?"

Athena's hand shot up. "Do you mean to say that these hero-guys represent real people? And our assignment is to make them do stuff down on Earth?"

"Yes, that's right," Mr. Cyclops said impatiently.

"How do we do that exactly?" asked Athena.

Everyone gasped so hard that it almost seemed as if all the air was being sucked out of the room.

"Are you for real?" Medusa whispered. "We learned Basic Mortal Manipulation in first grade!"

Mr. Cyclops's single eye blinked at Athena. "You must be the new student. You're going to have some catching up to do."

Athena slumped lower in her chair. She'd always been an A-plus student on Earth. Now, for the first time in her life, she felt dumb.

"I got Paris, a prince from the city of Troy. Who'd you get?" Aphrodite asked Athena after they'd both drawn from the helmet.

"Some Greek guy named Odysseus," said Athena, reading the card attached to her hero's neck.

"Ooh, he's cute," said Aphrodite, leaning across the aisle to peer at the statue.

Athena stared at the muscled, tanned mortal in her hand. He wore gold sandals laced up his calves and a white toga, and he had an adventurous look in his eyes. "I guess," she said. "I wonder what quest I should send him on?"

"I think I'll make Paris fall in love with somebody," said Aphrodite, drawing a heart on her card over the *i* in Paris's name.

"Falling in love isn't a quest," scoffed Medusa.

Aphrodite stiffened. "I wasn't talking to you."

"Sorry, Bubbles." Medusa snickered. "My mistake."

Aphrodite glared at her.

"Why'd she call you that?" asked Athena.

Aphrodite shrugged.

"Didn't you know?" Medusa butted in. "She was born from sea foam."

"And she never lets me forget it," said Aphrodite.

"What's wrong with sea foam? It's beautiful," said Athena.

"Think so?" asked Aphrodite, perking up.

Athena nodded, her eyes widening in surprise. How could someone so incredibly beautiful doubt she was pretty for even half a second?

Medusa started to say something else—probably

something mean—just as the school herald appeared in the doorway. In a clear voice that caught everyone's attention, he announced, "Will Athena—favorite daughter of Principal Zeus for all time and forevermore—please report to the office?"

The entire class turned to stare at Athena. She blushed in embarrassment. Favorite daughter? Was this her dad's idea of a joke? He hardly even *knew* her.

"Principal's pet," Medusa singsonged, softly so the teacher wouldn't hear.

"He sounds like he's in a good mood, anyway," said Aphrodite, giving Athena an encouraging smile.

What did she mean? Was Zeus usually a big grump? At least he'd used the word "please" instead of *commanding* her presence this time. That had to be a good sign, right?

45

As Athena stood up to go, she tripped over her bag. It fell open, and something rolled out onto the polished marble floor. Heads craned to see what it was, and there were giggles.

Ye gods! It was Woody—her wooden horse on wheels! What was he doing here? Had Pallas packed him in her bag, intending him to be a reminder of home?

Cheeks burning, Athena grabbed the horse by its red-and-white-striped reins. The little door in his side where she used to hide secret treasures like bird feathers and speckled rocks sprang open. She pushed it shut and rammed the toy back into her bag. Then she noticed a small shield-shaped mirror lying nearby that had also slid out. She and Pallas had each gotten one free when they'd gone to the grand opening of the Perseus Shield Market last year.

As Athena picked it up, she saw Medusa's smirk reflected on the mirror's silver surface. *I don't like you and you don't belong here,* the look on her face seemed to say.

Athena gulped. This was only her first class, but already it seemed she had made an enemy. Maybe she'd been too hasty in thinking she was going to fit in here on Mount Olympus any better than she had on Earth.

4

Dear Ol' Dad

ATHENA HOVERED AWKWARDLY IN ZEUS'S office doorway. His big head, with its wild red hair and curly beard, was bent over his desk as he chiseled a statue from a tall block of limestone. *Chink, chink, chink!*

"Well, don't just stand there!" he boomed when he finally noticed her.

Athena took a couple of steps into the room, then

stopped. There was nowhere else to go, because a tall file cabinet blocked her way. Her "dear ol' dad's" office looked like a tornado had hit it. Files, scrolls, maps, board games, and half-empty bottles of something labeled "Zeus Juice" were scattered everywhere. Discarded art projects carved from stone, wiggling plants, and a variety of chairs with big scorch marks on their cushions sat at odd angles as if positioned by a madman—or a mad*god.*

Zeus came out from behind his desk, and Athena stared at him in awe. He was nearly seven feet tall, with bulging muscles and piercing blue eyes. Wide, flat, golden bracelets encircled both of his wrists. She couldn't help shuddering when she noticed his thunderbolt belt buckle.

He lifted the file cabinet out of her way as if it

weighed no more than a footstool. Then he waved her into the chair across from his desk.

"Come! Sit!" he thundered.

Come? Sit? What did he think she was, his pet poodle? Eyeing the thunderbolt buckle, Athena sat.

Now that she was closer, she saw that the statue he'd been carving was actually a trophy of some kind. And it was the ugliest one she'd ever seen. It was probably supposed to be an eagle, or maybe a vulture or a pelican, holding bolts in its beak. But it was so badly crafted that it was impossible to tell. Though it was unfinished, he'd already carved some words on the front of the stone block the bird sat on:

GRAND PRIZE WINNER

OF THE

Zeus lowered himself back into the huge golden throne behind his desk. Leaning forward, he shoved the trophy aside and folded his hands on the desktop. "Now, what can I do you for?" he asked.

"Um," said Athena, feeling confused. "*You* asked *me* to come, remember?"

"Huh?"

"I'm Athena."

"Athena?"

"You know—your d-daughter?"

Zeus's face lit up like lightning had struck it. "Athena! My most favorite daughter in the whole wide universe. Welcome!"

He reached over the desk, grabbed her up, and gave her a big hug that squeezed all the breath out of her. Electricity fizzled from his fingertips, zapping her.

"Ow!" she yelped.

Suddenly Zeus got a weird look on his face. He set her back down and knocked the palm of his meaty hand against the side of his head. Tiny thunderbolts shot out from between his fingers in all directions, leaving steaming holes in a nearby chair, the wall, and a bottle of Zeus Juice.

"Stop it!" he grumped.

"Stop what?" Athena asked, gripping the arms of her chair nervously.

"I'll tell her already, Metis," he said. "You're such a headache sometimes!"

"Who are you talking to?" asked Athena, looking around to see if there was someone else in the room with them.

52

"Your mom," Zeus told her. "She says to tell you good luck on your first day, by the way."

Athena's heart did a little *thumpity-thump*. Well, of course she had a mom. Didn't everyone? But she'd thought her mother must be dead, since Zeus hadn't mentioned her in his letter. It had never occurred to her that she'd find *both* her parents on Mount Olympus.

"Where is she?" Athena asked, glancing eagerly around the room again.

"In here," Zeus said, tapping his forehead with a fingertip.

"Oh," said Athena, her eagerness giving way to disappointment. "I guess you must mean that she's still alive in your memories. Or something like that."

"Nonsense," said Zeus. "What I mean is that she's actually inside my skull. She's a fly, you know."

"A fly?" Athena echoed weakly, thinking she must've heard wrong. "As in a hairy-legged, two-winged, compound-eyed insect of the order Diptera?"

"Exactly right! And she's always bugging me about something." Zeus kicked back in his chair, propping his gold-sandaled feet on the desk. "But she's still a goddess, and she loves you. As much as an insect can, anyway."

Athena just stared at him, openmouthed. Talk about *weird*! This certainly put the odd in g*odd*ess!

"Better close your mouth. You'll catch flies." Zeus guffawed at his own joke, slapping his knee.

"But how can she actually live inside your, um . . . ," Athena babbled, gesturing at his forehead. She needed to know more, but hardly knew where to begin her questions. Wrapping her mind around the idea of having a fly as a mother wasn't going to be easy.

Zeus didn't seem to notice her confusion. "Well, Theeny," he went on, "now that I've gone to all the trouble of bringing you to Mount Olympus Academy, I hope you'll do me proud. The schoolwork here is harder than you're used to. Think you can handle it?"

Abandoning her attempt to come to terms with the revelation about her mother for the moment, Athena sat up straighter, trying to appear confident. "Sure."

"That's my goddessgirl!" Zeus boomed enthusiastically.

Athena rubbed her temple. She was getting a headache herself just listening to him. He was the loudest talker she'd ever met.

Just then a goddessgirl poked her head in the door. "Knock, knock," she said.

"Who's there?" Zeus replied, grinning as if he expected her to continue on with a joke.

"I'm Pheme. From Mr. Cyclops's class? He sent me to see if you were done with Athena. I'm supposed to take her back to Hero-ology."

Each word she spoke puffed from her lips like miniature smoke writing. Fascinating!

Zeus nodded. "Fine, fine. I think we're through here, aren't we, Theeny?"

"Well . . ." Athena had planned to ask if Pallas could visit her. And now she also had a thousand questions to ask about her mom.

But before she could get the words out, Zeus jumped up and roared, "Excellent! Now mind what I said—get out there and *learn*!" He punched the air with his fist as though to cheer her on.

Startled, Athena scrambled from her chair. "O-okay."

As she followed Pheme out of Zeus's office, he picked up his chisel again and started to work on his trophy, looking as if he'd already forgotten her. *Chink, chink, chink!*

"So what did you think of him?" Pheme asked once they were out in the hallway. Mesmerized by the sight of the cloudlike words coming from Pheme's mouth, Athena answered distractedly, "He's not what I expected, that's for sure."

"So you think he's kind of nutty?" Pheme puffed.

"No, that's not what I meant," said Athena.

"Then you think he's a blowhard?"

"No!" The girl was twisting her words. "He just

seems to have a lot on his mind, being principal of the school and King of the Gods and all."

"And being your *dad*, too," Pheme added slyly.

Suddenly Athena wondered how much of her conversation with Zeus Pheme had overheard. "Yeah. Um, did you have to wait for me outside his office very long?"

Pheme's eyes shifted away, and she toyed with her short, spiky orange hair.

Athena sighed. "Long enough to hear the stuff about my mom?"

The girl nodded, grinning. "Uh-huh. But don't worry, your secret's safe with me." She pressed her thumb and finger together at the corner of her orange-glossed lips and twisted them, as if turning a key to lock them shut.

Athena smiled. "Thanks. I appreciate that."

The end-of-period lyrebell sounded as they reached Mr. Cyclops's classroom.

"See you later," said Pheme. "Gotta meet up with some friends." With that, she ran over to several goddessgirls at the back of the room—a group that included Medusa.

As Athena gathered her scrolls and bag to lug to her second-period class, she saw the girls whispering with their heads close together. Looking up, Medusa smirked at her.

"What is Pheme the goddess of?" Athena asked, catching up with Aphrodite on the way out of the room.

Aphrodite wrinkled her nose. "Gossip."

Athena gulped. That didn't sound good at all! If the other students hadn't already known her mom was a fly, it wouldn't be long before they found out. Could things get any worse?

"I've got my favorite class next—Beauty-ology!" Aphrodite told her as the two of them stepped into the hall. "How about you?"

"Beast-ology," said Athena.

"Look out—I hear the teacher is a total monster!" a godboy quipped, pushing past them. *Squish, squish.* It was Poseidon.

Athena laughed, and he smiled over his shoulder at her.

For some reason, Aphrodite looked stunned that he'd paid attention to them. "Poseidon is one of the most popular godboys in school," she whispered close to Athena's ear.

Slowing, Poseidon spun around to walk backward

alongside them. "I'm in Beast-ology next too," he told Athena. "Want me to show you the way?"

"Sure, thanks," said Athena.

Still looking amazed, Aphrodite gave her a little wave. "I'm off. Beauty-ology is in the other direction, so I'll see you later."

"Okay," said Athena.

When Poseidon turned to lead her to their next class, he bumped into Medusa. "Oh, sorry."

"No problem," Medusa said in a sweet voice.

Shocked at the change in her, Athena did a double take. Medusa was staring at Poseidon with a dreamy, love-struck expression. He responded by shooting her a blinding white smile. What a flirt!

But Athena forgot all about Medusa as she and Poseidon got to their next class and passed the teacher in the doorway. "Welcome to Beassstology. I'm Missster Ladon," he told them. Licks of fire flew from his lips with each word. A couple of embers floated down to land on Athena's scrolls.

Smacking the papyrus before it could catch fire, Athena managed to introduce herself in return.

"Mr. Ladon's got the worst dragon breath of any teacher in school," Poseidon joked as she chose a seat. Grinning, he took the desk right behind hers. Immediately a bunch of goddessgirls rushed for the empty seats nearest to him, each vying for his attention.

Athena couldn't help feeling amused. Did every girl in the academy have a crush on him? Pallas would be happy to know he was as cute as she'd hoped, but she might not like knowing what a flirt he was. At least he wasn't stuck-up.

5

Yambrosia

AFTER BEAST-OLOGY, IT WAS LUNCHTIME. IN the cafeteria, an eight-armed, octopus-like lunch lady served the line of students from orange clay bowls decorated with black silhouetted figures. Athena didn't recognize any of the foods being served and didn't know what to choose. What was yambrosia? Or nectaroni? Or cheese styx?

The big celestial salad didn't look too weird. She chose that and a carton of nectar to drink. And last but not least, she selected a big cookie from a basket that was full of them.

Athena took her tray into the lunchroom. She didn't see Aphrodite, so she headed for an open spot at a nearby table.

"Do you hear a buzzing noise, Sthenno?" a snarky voice asked as she sat down.

Oh, no! She'd chosen the same table where Medusa and her two sisters sat! Athena ignored them, hoping they'd decide to ignore her, too.

No such luck.

One of Medusa's sisters tilted her head, like she was listening to something. "Sounds sort of like a mosquito, don't you think, Euryale?"

"No, more like a bee," her sister Sthenno answered.

"Or—I know—a *fly*!" said Medusa.

Pheme must have blabbed what she'd heard in Zeus's office!

"Cute," Athena muttered. "Very. I wonder if there's anything about bullies in the *Goddessgirl Guide*?" Pointedly, she pulled the pink scroll from her bag.

Grinning nastily, Medusa stood with her tray. "C'mon, Sthenno, Euryale. Let's go find another table. For some reason, this one's giving me a headache."

"Maybe you swallowed Athena's mom," said Sthenno.

Giggling like that was the funniest joke they'd ever heard, all three left for another table.

Hoping no one had noticed how rudely she'd been abandoned, Athena set the pink scroll aside and finished her salad. Then she opened the *Guide* to take a look. A delicious perfumey smell drifted from it as she unrolled the pink papyrus.

The first chapter told her a lot about gods and goddesses. It said that goddess moms and god dads were very busy and sometimes forgot all about their kids for years at a time. Well, that explained about Zeus not contacting her until now.

Athena ran a finger down the scroll. "Gods and goddesses stay immortal by eating a divine confection called ambrosia and by sipping nectar," she read. So that's what the fountains of Mount Olympus spouted!

She kept reading, but no matter how much she unrolled the slender scroll, it never seemed to end. It was some kind of magic, she realized, that allowed a lot of information to fit within a small scroll of papyrus.

She skimmed partway through, noticing that the *Guide* also listed school rules—which included no bullying, a dress code, and ways to smite mortals. She was going to love learning how to do that. Though, of course, she'd never smite any nice mortals like Pallas.

Sighing, she wished Pallas were here right now. Then she'd have someone friendly to talk to. Shoving the pink scroll aside, Athena pulled out a ball of yellow yarn. Knitting relaxed her, and it would help disguise the fact that she was a loser with no friends. The soft *click, click* of her needles was a comforting sound.

When lunch period was nearly over, she remembered the cookie. Finding it under the pink scroll, she tore off the wrapper and bit into it.

Instantly, a small, dramatic voice announced, "You'll be famous."

"What?" Athena looked around, her eyes wide. No one was near.

"Who said that?" she asked. But no one answered. She took another bite.

"You'll be famous," the little voice said again. It was coming from the cookie!

Athena dropped it on the table, eyeing it warily. "Um, are you alive?"

Silence.

Leaning closer, she read the cookie's wrapper: ORACLE-O COOKIE. Oracles told fortunes. It was a fortune cookie! A talking one, apparently. She got up to throw away her trash, unsure what to do with the cookie. Fortunes were always so silly, but she couldn't eat the cookie now that she knew it talked.

"Well, so long," she said uncertainly, leaving it on

the table. On the way out of the lunchroom, a poster on the wall caught her eye.

INVENTION FAIR

INVENT SOMETHING THE GREEKS ADORE, AND

YOU'LL BE FAMOUS!

(PLUS YOU'LL GET EXTRA CREDIT.)

ENTRIES DUE: FRIDAY

JUDGES: GREEK MORTALS

You'll be famous? What a coincidence that those were the exact words her fortune cookie had just spoken.

Athena glanced back at her table just in time to see a froggy-looking lunch lady unroll her long, sticky tongue and flick Athena's half-eaten cookie into her mouth. She went on to other tables, eating bits of leftover food here and there, and then wiping the tabletops.

Ugh! Athena returned her gaze to the poster. Below it was a stack of entry blanks. She peeled one off. Maybe she'd enter.

Just then she heard a familiar *squish, squish* sound behind her. Poseidon.

"Planning to enter?" he asked her.

Athena took a step back. The three-pronged trident he was holding was dripping on her shoes. Had he been swimming? "Maybe," she said. "You?"

"Sure. And I'm in it to win." He cocked his head, considering her. "Rumor has it you're pretty brainy. If you want, I'll let you be my assistant. You can help me with my idea."

He'd *let* her be *his* assistant? Suddenly Poseidon didn't seem quite as handsome anymore. "Thanks, but I've got my own ideas," Athena said, a little annoyed. "By the way, your pitchfork's dripping," she added, purposely calling it by the wrong name.

"It's a trident!" he said, tapping the tip of its long handle on the floor for emphasis.

"Whatever," Athena said lightly. "See ya." Spotting Aphrodite among a group of girls nearby, she stuffed the entry form in her pocket and headed toward her.

"Hi," said Aphrodite. "Thinking of trying out?"

"For what?" asked Athena.

"Goddessgirl Squad." When Athena looked blank, Aphrodite pointed toward a sign-up sheet posted on the wall. "Mount Olympus Academy is the home of the Fightin' Titans. The GG Squad cheers them on at the Olympic Games. Chariot and foot races. Javelin and discus throwing. Wrestling. You know, stuff like that."

One of Aphrodite's friends—the dark-haired god-dessgirl beside her—began to wave her arms in a choreographed move, no easy feat with a bow and a quiver slung over her shoulder. She burst into a cheer: "We're mighty! We're fightin'! We're the mighty, fightin' Titans! Woo-hoo!"

"Woo-woo!" The three dogs by her side—a blood-hound, a greyhound, and a beagle—howled along with her as she did a high kick.

"Wow, that was great!" said Athena.

"Thanks. Persephone made that one up," the girl said modestly, referring to the red-haired goddessgirl next to her.

Aphrodite introduced the girl with the dogs as Artemis, and the girl with the curly red hair as Perse-phone.

"You should try out. We could use some new blood on the squad," Persephone told Athena in a soft voice.

She was so pale she looked like *she* could use some new blood herself, thought Athena. "I don't know . . . ," she began.

"You'll get to hang out with the cute guys on the Titans team," Aphrodite said, smiling and arching one perfect eyebrow. "Poseidon is one of them."

"You've got a one-track mind," Artemis teased, gently elbowing Aphrodite. "Who cares about dumb ol' godboys? I joined the squad to keep in shape."

"I'm not sure I've got time for any extracurriculars," said Athena doubtfully. And she didn't care about hanging out with Poseidon, that was for sure. He was much too full of himself.

"Being on the GG Squad looks good on your academic record," Persephone coaxed.

Zeus would probably like it if she made the squad, Athena mused. And she really wanted to make friends with these nice girls. Still, a tiny part of her wondered if entering the Invention Fair, going out for GG Squad, and keeping up with her regular class assignments might be too big of a load for her first few months at school. Besides, according to the poster, squad tryouts were after school tomorrow!

Ignoring her misgivings, she heard herself say, "Well I guess I could at least give it a shot." Picking up the quill pen, she wrote her name on the sign-up sheet.

6

Roomie

"A RE YOU MY ROOMMATE?" A FAMILIAR VOICE

asked.

Athena looked up from the built-in desk in her new

dorm room to see Pandora standing in the doorway.

Oh, no.

She'd known she would be sharing the room. One

of the closets had already been full of clothes when

she'd come upstairs to the dorm after her last class that day. But until this moment she hadn't known who her roommate would be.

"Guess so," Athena said, trying to smile. It wasn't that she didn't like Pandora. It was just that she talked too much.

"Got a lot of homework, huh?" asked Pandora as she tossed her school things onto her bed. Their room was small, with an identical bed, desk, and closet on each side. The bathroom and showers were down the hall.

Athena nodded. "There should be a law against homework on the first day of school."

"Wouldn't that be cool?" Pandora came closer and craned her neck for a peek. "What are you working on?"

Stop being so nosy, Athena wanted to say. But instead she replied, "Something for the Invention Fair."

"Really? What?"

Athena sighed. She and Pallas had stayed up late her last night on Earth, and her first day of school had been tiring. "Um, Pandora, I've got a lot of work to do, catching up and all, so . . ."

"Oh, sure, I understand." Pandora was quiet for about half a second, then she offered, "Need any help?"

"No, thanks," Athena answered automatically. She didn't want anyone to think she couldn't keep up with her workload. "Don't you have any homework?"

"Me? Nope, I finished it in study hall," said Pandora.

If a mortal like Pandora can keep up, I should be able to, thought Athena. Too bad she hadn't taken a study hall instead of one of her classes, though.

Without asking first, Pandora picked up the stack of sketches Athena had set on the bed and began looking through them. She studied the top one—a drawing of an oval. She turned it upside down and then right side up again. "What's this?"

"Those are my invention ideas, for the school contest. I call that one an olive," said Athena. "It's a little fruit about the size of the tip of your thumb. I made it to jazz up the celestial salad the lunch ladies make, to add something a little salty and different. I haven't drawn the tree it grows on yet, but it'll be evergreen, with pretty silver-green leaves on branches you can weave together to make crowns."

"Hmm. I'm sure it's tasty, but I'm not really a salad person," said Pandora. She frowned as she went on to the next sketch. "Why did you draw a picture of Poseidon's new pitchfork?"

"I didn't." Athena moved closer to point out the differences. "This invention's called a rake, and it has way more prongs than his trident."

"But what does it do? Slay Chimeras or calm the Furies?"

"No," said Athena, beginning to feel a little embarrassed. "It's for mortals to use for farming and yard work. I was thinking about all the leaves and hay I saw in the farm fields when I was flying up to Mount Olympus this morning. That's what gave me the idea. My rake could sweep those up better than any broom."

Pandora wrinkled her nose, obviously unimpressed. She probably thought hay rakes were too boring to win.

Pandora picked up another drawing. "What's this one?"

"I call it a ship," said Athena, crossing her fingers that she would like at least one of her ideas. "It floats in the sea like a papyrus sailboat or a reed raft. Only it's bigger, so it holds lots of people."

Pandora considered it, cocking her head. "I'll give this one a maybe."

Athena nodded, feeling a little let down. She'd thought her inventions were pretty good, but Pandora's lack of enthusiasm was discouraging.

Knock, knock.

"Who is it?" called Pandora. Dropping the sketches on Athena's bed, she crossed the room to throw open the door. Aphrodite stood just outside in the hall.

"Where did you come from?" asked Pandora, poking her head out to glance up and down the hallway.

"Nine doors down," Aphrodite said as she stepped inside. "Artemis has the room next to mine."

"You're not sharing?" asked Pandora.

Aphrodite shook her head. "She needed a bed for her dogs, and I needed more closet space. So we each got our own rooms."

"What about Persephone?" asked Pandora, pulling her head back in. "Is she on our floor too?"

Aphrodite smiled at Athena, raising her brows. There was sympathy in her gaze. Pandora's questions probably got on *her* nerves too, Athena realized. She smiled back, glad someone else understood. "Persephone is living at home with her mom this year," Aphrodite told Pandora.

At the mention of "home," Athena felt a pang of loneliness even in the midst of the excitement of making new friends.

"Artemis and I thought you might be feeling a little

homesick," said Aphrodite as if reading her mind. "So we've decided to have a 'Welcome to MOA' party."

Before she could add another word there was a clatter in the hallway, and Artemis rushed in. Her three dogs bounced in behind her, tails wagging. She dropped a bowl of chips on Pandora's bed, then hurried to open the room's large window. She didn't seem to notice when her dogs began gobbling the snacks.

"Come look!" she shouted. "Someone's raining all kinds of weird stuff down on Earth. It's the wildest thing I've ever seen!"

All four girls crowded at the window to gaze outside. A storm of objects that looked suspiciously like those in Athena's sketches had appeared out of nowhere.

They whirled high in the air within a tornado for a few seconds. Then they began to fall, one by one. As gravity pulled them toward Earth, lights in villages and cities far below began to flicker on. Voices drifted upward through the clouds, reaching their ears.

"Ow!"

"Stop!"

"Ow! Ow!"

"Why are the gods angry with us?"

"What's going on? Whose voices are those?" asked Athena.

"Mortals," said Aphrodite. "They're complaining so loudly, we can hear it all the way up here."

"Whoa! Somebody at the academy is going to be in trouble for this prank," said Artemis.

Pandora's eyes got big, and she turned to Athena. "When you were inventing stuff and making your sketches, did you block your brainstorming?"

Athena shook her head. *Block her brainstorming?* What was that supposed to mean? "I didn't know I was supposed to," she stammered. "I mean, I don't know how."

"Uh-oh," said Aphrodite, looking worried. "Where are these sketches?"

Athena pointed toward the stack on her bed.

Artemis had already discovered them and was flipping through them. "Doggone! These look exactly like the objects in the storm."

"You should never make sketches without bespelling them to stay put on the page first," Aphrodite cautioned Athena.

"WHO'S DOING ALL THIS BRAINSTORM-ING?" a voice boomed from the courtyard below.

"Zeus is out there!" whispered Pandora, her eyes

wide. At the mention of the principal's name, Artemis's dogs glanced up with interest for a second, but then went back to chomping snacks.

Athena peeked outside. Zeus was standing in the courtyard, with his fists at his hips. He did not look happy.

Nervously, she waved a hand to get his attention. "Umm . . . Dad, er, Principal Zeus! I think I did it. I'm sorry!"

"Theeny? Is that you?" roared Zeus, looking up at her in outrage. "You can't go around whipping up a storm of ideas willy-nilly! Don't you know that everything a goddessgirl does affects mortals down there on Earth? There are rules, for godness' sake!"

His loud voice bounced off the walls, echoing around the courtyard and throughout the school.

"But I didn't know," Athena called back.

"It's all in the *Goddessgirl Guide*. You should have memorized all two thousand and one rules by now," he called back.

"But I just got here today," Athena protested. "I haven't had time—"

"NO EXCUSES!" Zeus boomed, so loud this time that the mirror rattled on the wall. Muttering to himself, he stomped back inside the academy.

Just then Athena noticed that there were tons of students in the courtyard. Even more hung out of the doors and windows of the school building, craning to listen. They'd heard everything. How embarrassing! She slid down the wall to sit on the floor below the window. "I stink at being a goddessgirl," she moaned.

"Don't worry," said Artemis, trying to cheer her up.

"Zeus's bark is worse than his bite. He's always giving me demerits when my hounds get too rambunctious, but then he forgets all about it." She knelt down and gave her three dogs a group hug. "Doesn't he, guys?"

"Really?" Athena asked hopefully.

When the others nodded, she felt a little better. After Artemis went for a fresh bowl of chips and ambrosia dip, the four girls sat two on a bed, opened bottles of nectar, and ate snacks.

"I'm sure everything seems hard now, but you'll pick it up in no time," Aphrodite assured Athena.

"My first semester here at the academy was a fiasco," said Artemis, tossing chips to her hounds one by one. "I couldn't get the hang of Spell-ology for the longest time. I kept sneezing and turning everyone into dogs. Or fleas."

"Remember what I did back in fifth grade?" said Pandora, rolling her eyes.

"Oh, yeah! Who could forget?" said Aphrodite.

"What?" asked Athena.

"I accidentally opened a box of disasters in Mr. Epimetheus's class, and most of them escaped to Earth," Pandora admitted. "I thought Zeus was going to send me back home for sure. Or worse. But he didn't."

If Pandora hadn't gotten expelled for such a big mistake, surely Zeus wouldn't expel her for her brainstorming blunder, thought Athena. Although she missed Pallas, she didn't want to be banished to Triton Junior High again.

She was enjoying her new friends and her new classes here at MOA too much. At the same time she felt a little guilty for having so much fun. But Pallas would be making new friends too. She'd understand. Wouldn't she?

Hours later, after Aphrodite and Artemis returned to their rooms and Pandora had gone to sleep, Athena stared tiredly at all the homework she still had to do. She would've given up on the Invention Fair altogether, but now she felt like she owed the mortals for what she'd accidentally done to them that afternoon.

No matter what the other girls said, she still thought she stunk at being a goddessgirl—at least so far. Maybe things would go better tomorrow.

She sat at her desk and got to work.

7

Drowning

THE NEXT MORNING ATHENA OVERSLEPT.

Not a good start to her second day. Then, while dashing to class, she tripped over something on the stairs and fell, skinning her knee. She picked up the object to examine it, then tucked it in her bag. It was a little ship—one of the inventions that had magically appeared when she'd brainstormed yesterday. Most of them had fallen to Earth, but this one apparently hadn't made it that far.

Mr. Cyclops gave her the stink-eye when she slipped into Hero-ology class late, but at least he didn't scold her in front of everyone. For some reason, all the desks had been pushed against the walls on two sides of the room today. A long table stood in the middle of the floor, and a three-dimensional map covered its entire top. The teacher and students were all standing around it.

"You'll each find your hero somewhere on this map," Mr. Cyclops was saying. He'd collected the little statues yesterday at the end of class, explaining that they were never to leave the room.

When Athena got close enough, she saw that the huge map was very realistic. There were roads, valleys, villages, and castles with moats around them. The tallest mountain stood nearly a foot high, and strange, scaly beasts peeked from the seas and oceans.

"What did I miss?" Athena whispered to Aphrodite.

"We're beginning our quests," Aphrodite whispered back. "I made Paris fall in love with a pretty mortal named Helen. He just took her to his fortress in Troy to show her around. Isn't that romantic?" She sighed blissfully.

"Smooth move, Bubbles," Medusa said sarcastically. "In case you hadn't noticed, someone else was already in love with Helen. My hero—King Menelaus from Sparta."

"He was?" Aphrodite looked sweetly mystified. "Oops."

Medusa called Mr. Cyclops over to complain. His eye studied the map carefully, but he didn't seem mad about what had happened. Instead he said, "This is somewhat irregular, Aphrodite, but I like that you were able to set up roadblocks to success for two heroes at the same time."

Anyone else would have gotten in trouble for making such a mistake, thought Athena. But Aphrodite was so glamorous and nice, you just *had* to excuse her, no matter what she did. Unless, of course, you were Medusa, who was now looking rather grumpy.

"Remember, you'll all be graded on the creativity of the quests you design, and also on your ability to get your heroes out of trouble," Mr. Cyclops told the class. "So don't make things too easy on your heroes. They must be tested in ways that prove they're heroic. Otherwise they'd just be *ordinary* mortals."

Athena thought about that as she searched for her

Odysseus figure. Where in the world had Mr. Cyclops put him? She finally found him standing on an island called Ithaca. It was in the Ionian Sea, west of Greece. She picked him up by the head, using two fingers.

Aphrodite gasped. "Don't hold him like that. You're probably giving him a horrible headache."

"Oh! Sorry," said Athena. Remembering what Zeus had said about how everything goddessgirls did had an effect on mortals, she carefully set Odysseus in her palm instead.

"Hmm. Where should you go, little hero?" she wondered. Considering the map, she stifled a yawn. She'd fallen asleep last night in the middle of her reading assignment, but the last thing she'd read was that a quest should involve excitement, action, and travel.

The map was like a game board, she realized as she

studied it. Each hero would be working toward a goal, but also trying to outdo the others. And the godboys and goddessgirls who manipulated the figures would each be graded on how well their hero succeeded. Sort of like a chess game, only more interesting—and with tangible results.

Athena yawned again. She was so tired it was hard to think. Resting her elbows on the edge of the map, she put her chin in her empty hand, just for a minute.

"Careful—you'll drown him!" someone shouted a while later.

"What?" Athena awoke with a start and looked around in surprise. Her head had been lying on her forearms, which were folded on the edge of the map. She'd been sleeping standing up!

"Fish him out!" Mr. Cyclops urged. "Hurry!" The whole class was staring at her in horror.

Athena looked down at the map just in time to see Odysseus sink into the Mediterranean Sea. She must've dropped him when she fell asleep!

"This is *real* water?" She reached for him, grabbing his foot in the nick of time. Something under the water's surface nibbled at her finger. She bent to look closer. A grinning sea monster about ten inches long splashed out and licked her nose.

"Ew!" she said, jerking back. Not only were the seas and oceans real, the beasts that lurked in them were too!

Holding Odysseus in one fist, Athena quickly grabbed the bag at her feet with her other hand. After digging around in it a minute, she pulled out the little ship she'd found on the stairs on the way to class.

"Here you go," she said, plopping it into the Mediter-ranean Sea and setting Odysseus inside it. "This ship is just the thing to get you where you're going. Once I decide where that is."

"Good save," murmured Aphrodite.

"Thanks," she said. "But I almost drowned poor Odysseus. What a terrible thing to do to a poor, unsus-pecting mortal!"

"Don't worry. You'll get better at this stuff after a while," said Aphrodite.

But what if I don't? worried Athena. *What if I make a mistake and do something like that to another mortal someday?* Like Pallas, for instance. That would be awful!

Athena was beginning to think supernatural powers were nothing but a big pain. Every little mistake the gods and goddesses made could cause trouble. And the whole world was watching their every move.

So was Mr. Cyclops. Although he only had one eye, it seemed to notice everything.

"You'd better get going," Medusa told her haughtily. "King Menelaus just commanded Odysseus to bring Helen back from Troy."

"You—he can't do that," Athena protested.

Aphrodite gently elbowed her. "Yes, she can," she warned.

"But why?"

"Because my king is your hero's boss, that's why," Medusa informed her snidely. "Didn't you do our reading assignment?"

"Must have missed that part," said Athena. There was no way she was going to admit to Medusa that she'd fallen asleep in the middle of reading her text-scroll last night.

"You're only doing this to Athena to spite me, aren't you?" Aphrodite said to Medusa.

Medusa shrugged. "So? If Athena wants a good grade, her hero has to follow my orders."

With a huge sigh, Athena turned toward the map again. "Okay. I'm going, I'm going." With one finger-tip, she steered Odysseus's ship through the Mediter-ranean Sea toward Troy. How was she going to get Helen away from Paris, as Medusa had ordered, without making Aphrodite mad?

Meanwhile Poseidon, who must have overheard them, was busy helping his hero build walls around Troy to keep Odysseus out.

Every time Athena tried to set Odysseus's ship on

an even course, Poseidon blew great puffs of air along the water's surface, rocking the ship and pushing it backward.

"You sure enjoy making waves," Athena said, glaring at him.

"Yep. As I told you yesterday, I like to win." Poseidon flashed a grin.

Medusa stepped between them, shooting Athena a mean look before turning to face him. "How did you ever build that wall so fast?" she asked him. "You're *sooo* clever."

Poseidon beamed at her. "Aren't I, though? But building a wall is easy. Watch." Basking in her flattery, he began showing her how to construct a clay wall.

Why, she'd deliberately drawn away Poseidon's attention, Athena realized. Because she was jealous!

It turned out that Medusa's king was very power-ful. He sent more heroes to help Odysseus, and before long, everyone's heroes were fighting one another. Half of the class, including Aphrodite and Poseidon, had been assigned heroes on the Trojan team. They were all rooting for Paris's side to win.

The other half of the class, including Athena and Medusa, was part of the Greek team, rooting for Odysseus and King Menelaus's side to win. Too bad Mr. Cyclops wouldn't let Medusa and Aphrodite trade heroes, thought Athena. Then Medusa could work at Poseidon's side, just the way she probably wanted, and Athena and Aphrodite could be on the same team.

The fighting heated up. Suddenly Athena wasn't worrying about her grades. Or about Mr. Cyclops. She was worrying about her hero!

"We've got to find a way to end this battle," she told her teammates.

Medusa folded her arms. "I'm not giving in to Aphrodite, if that's what you have in mind. I won't be happy until my king gets Helen back from Paris."

"Okay then, I have another idea." Athena opened her bag and pulled out the toy horse Pallas had stowed. Thank godness she'd been too tired to unpack last night.

"Meet Woody," she announced to the whole class, setting him just outside the gates of Troy. She pulled the red ribbon from her Hero-ology textscroll and tied it in a bow around his neck, as if he were a gift.

"Why did you put him at our gates?" Poseidon asked suspiciously.

"He's a going-away present," Athena replied casually.

"A present?" Aphrodite echoed.

Athena hated to fib to her new friend, but she wanted to win this game and do well in class just as much as Poseidon did—maybe even more so. She turned away and began loading her team's heroes onto the little ship.

"So you're just going to give up?" asked Medusa, curling her lip in disgust.

"At least it will end the fighting," Athena said, loudly enough that everyone would hear.

Then to Medusa and the rest of her team, she murmured softly, "Just trust me. I have a plan, but there's no time to explain."

"Trust you?" hissed Medusa. "Ha! You're just giving up because Aphrodite's your friend. And because you're crushing on Poseidon."

"That's not it at all," Athena whispered. The ship was full of heroes now, so she pushed it off to sail away toward the Mediterranean.

Still looking like he smelled a rat, Poseidon nevertheless moved his hero figure toward the fortress gate.

"Wait!" Aphrodite said. "Are you certain we want this gift?"

"Sure, why not?" Before she could stop him, he opened the gate, grabbed Woody's rope, and tugged him inside the walls. Then he slammed the gate shut again and locked it behind them.

Ping! Ping! Ping!

The whole class groaned—even Mr. Cyclops. Just when things were getting interesting, the period had ended. They would all have to wait till tomorrow to find out what would happen next.

8

Three Cheers

AFTER SCHOOL THAT DAY, ATHENA MET
Aphrodite, Artemis, and Persephone on the coliseum
field behind the academy for Goddessgirl Squad
tryouts. Medusa, her sisters, and three dozen other
goddessgirls and mortals were there trying out
too, but Pandora had decided to go out for the flag
marching team instead. Nearby, the godboys and

goddessgirls on the Titans team were practicing for the Olympic games that would be held throughout the year.

Athena snapped open her gold fans. Along with the entire group, she made pyramids and practiced spins and splits. For the past two hours, they'd all been learning dance moves and chants.

Behold! Behold!

We're Fightin' Titan BOLD!

Behold! Behold!

We're Fightin' Titan GOLD!

When Coach Nike and her nine assistants, the Muses, began taking the girls in smaller clusters for the final squad tryouts, Athena decided to talk to Medusa. It wasn't something she wanted to do, but perhaps if she explained about Woody and her Hero-ology plan, Medusa would stop seeing her as an enemy. Not that they'd ever be best friends!

Athena waited until her group, Medusa's group, and some others who weren't up till the end went to the nectar fountain for drinks. Then Athena approached Medusa and her sisters.

As she did, a soft cheer broke out among the triplets, stopping her cold. Everyone in the fountain line turned to look.

"Give me an *F*!" chanted Medusa.

"Give me an *L*!" chanted Sthenno.

"Give me a *Y*!" chanted Euryale.

"What's that spell?" asked Medusa.

"Athena's mom!" her sisters shouted.

Athena's face turned red. But the horror wasn't over.

ZZZZ. Making buzzing noises, the triplets whipped out flyswatters they'd tucked in their belts. They must've been planning this even before tryouts, Athena realized. How mean! Waving the swatters in choreographed moves, the girls launched into a little skit.

"Got a headache! Me, oh my!"

(Stomp, swat. Stomp, swat, swat.)

"How to stop it? Swat that fly!"

(Stomp, swat. Stomp, swat, swat.)

Though they were too far away for the coach to hear, the other girls in the drink line could hear them just fine.

"Stop picking on Athena," said Artemis, stepping up to them.

"Yeah," said Aphrodite, joining her.

"Nobody can help who their parents are," said

Persephone, standing alongside the other two to form a wall of goddessgirls between them and Athena.

"C'mon, let's go back to the others," said Aphrodite. She, Artemis, and Persephone linked arms with Athena, and they headed back to the tryout area.

"Thanks, you guys," Athena told them, still a little shaken and pink faced.

"Our pleasure," said Aphrodite.

"Yeah," agreed Artemis.

"Any time," added Persephone.

It was nice of them to stand up for her, thought Athena. Still, the mean skit had rattled her. And now it was their group's turn to perform in the final tryouts. If she messed up, she'd ruin her new friends' chances at making the GG Squad.

Just as the four of them stepped up to try out,

Poseidon threw his trident across the field. It soared in a high arc through the air, like a javelin.

Quickly, on Aphrodite's signal, the four goddess-girls launched into a chant:

> *Boom Boom, thunderation,*
> *Send that trident on vacation!*
> *Woo-hoo!*

Athena and her friends swished their sparkly fans. Then, as one, they whispered, "Shift." As they spoke each of them shape-shifted, sprouting a set of glossy white wings at their shoulder blades. Holding hands, they rose a dozen feet into the air. Gently flapping their wings, they held up six fans in alignment, each one painted with one letter of their school's team name: TITANS.

Then they swooped low toward the field again. As they touched down, like magic, their wings melted away. Shape-shifting had proven amazingly easy for Athena. She'd gotten it right on her third try. In fact, the GG Squad was turning out to be way more fun than she'd expected.

As he retrieved his trident, pulling its prongs from where they'd stuck in the grassy field when it landed, Poseidon shot Athena a huge smile. "Thanks!"

He'd thrown farther than any of the other godboys. Triumphant, he jogged back to his teammates.

Meanwhile, Medusa turned to see who he'd smiled at. When she saw it was Athena, her green face turned a purple shade that was not at all attractive.

"Godboy moocher!" she hissed when Athena drew near.

"I didn't mooch anything," Athena protested in surprise. Did Medusa think she'd made up the cheer for Poseidon? It had been Aphrodite's idea to show support for him and the whole Titan team.

"Humph! We'll see how you like it when the tables are turned!" Medusa stormed off. Her sisters followed, glaring at Athena.

Athena turned to her friends. "What did she mean by that?"

"Who knows?" said Aphrodite. "But take my advice and try to stay out of her way. She aces Revenge-ology every year."

"And she's in the accelerated class," Artemis noted worriedly.

"What a mess," said Persephone.

"Yeah," agreed Athena, shaking her head in bewilderment. "Medusa's crushing on Poseidon, and she thinks *he's* crushing on me."

Aphrodite gave her an exasperated look. "She's right—he is. Trust me, I have a sense about matters of the heart. Poseidon's probably never come across a girl who didn't fall for him right away. That's why he's trying so hard with you. You're a challenge!"

"He just likes to flirt!" objected Athena. "With every girl in sight!"

Artemis rolled her eyes. "All this yucky romance stuff is going to make me barf. Since we're finished, I'm gonna go get my dogs some chow." She headed over to unleash them from the stone bleachers.

Now that the last group had finished trying out,

Coach Nike and the nine Muses left the field to tally the results and decide who'd made the Goddess Squad. They told everyone that the results would be posted later in the week.

"Hey!" someone shouted, as the godboys on the field finished their practice. "I just heard that our Trojan and Greek heroes are fighting it out in Hero-ology without us!"

"This I have to see!" said Athena. She, Aphrodite, and several others raced to Mr. Cyclops's classroom. The shades had been pulled at the end of the day, leaving the room dim. Sure enough, their heroes were duking it out within the gates of Troy.

Athena's wooden horse still stood inside the fortress, but now the little door in its side was open. It had been so well concealed that no one on the Trojan team had noticed it—until now.

Poseidon peeked inside the door. "A secret compartment!"

"Well, what do you know?" said Aphrodite. Her eyes widened in surprise.

"The horse wasn't a gift at all. It was a trick, wasn't it?" said Poseidon.

"Yep," said Athena. "You see, not all our heroes got aboard the ship that sailed away during class. I hid Odysseus and a few others inside the horse. While we were out on the field, they staged a sneak attack and stole Helen. They sent her back to King Menelaus in Sparta."

Poseidon looked shocked that he'd been bested by a girl, but Athena didn't care. She turned toward

Aphrodite. "I'm sorry I spoiled your plans for Paris and Helen's happily-ever-after."

"That's okay," said Aphrodite, shrugging. "It's just a class assignment. I think your idea was clever!"

"No hard feelings?" asked Athena.

"Of course not," said Aphrodite. "This is the most exciting thing to happen in Hero-ology since first grade. When Mr. Cyclops hears about your ruse, he'll be dancing in his sandals."

"If he can find them, that is," someone joked. As was widely known, their teacher liked to kick off his sandals in class, and he always seemed to be losing them.

As she left the room, Athena decided that her second day at MOA had been a whole lot better than her first. Her trick in Hero-ology had worked, she'd done well in the GG Squad tryouts, and despite Medusa and her sisters' embarrassing fly routine, she now had friends to come to her rescue. She smiled to herself. It was just possible that this day marked a turning point in her new life at Mount Olympus Academy.

9

Missing

"ONE OF MY INVENTIONS IS MISSING," ATHENA said the next morning as she pawed through the papers on her dorm room desk.

"Which one?" asked Aphrodite. Studying her reflection in Athena's mirror, she tried out different ways of tying the belt on her blue-and-silver-patterned chiton. She and Artemis had come to hang out with Athena until it was time for their first class. Pandora had left early, saying she needed to drop off some scrolls at the library before classes started.

"I named it Snarkypoo," said Athena, as she continued to search.

A giggle burst from Artemis before she could smother it. "Snarkypoo? That's the goofiest name I ever heard!" Her dogs snuffled too, almost as if they were laughing along with her.

Athena ignored them. She stuck her head in the bottom of her closet, then opened every drawer in her desk, and even flipped over her mattress. Finally she gave a frustrated huff and dropped into her chair. "It was right here on my desk. What could've happened to it? The Invention Fair is tomorrow!"

Aphrodite peered over Athena's shoulder at the

jumble of papers and scrolls on her desk. "I almost hate to ask, but what exactly *is* Snarkypoo?"

"Just shampoo. After someone uses it, any snarky words they think of turn to stone in their brain before they can be spoken." Athena grinned slightly. "I invented it with Medusa in mind."

"I like it!" said Aphrodite. Leaning closer, she pointed to a word on the list Athena had made of all her inventions. "But didn't you misspell it?"

"Oh, no!" said Athena, after bending closer to examine her list. "You're right! I wrote *Snakey*poo by mistake."

Artemis and her dogs laughed again.

Athena glared at them. "It's not funny." Then she found herself chuckling too. "Well, I guess it is a little. But what could've happened to it?" She ducked under her desk, digging through her bag for a third time.

"Maybe it *slithered* away," Aphrodite teased.

Athena stood again, shaking her head. "No, it couldn't have done that. At least I don't think it could." She frowned thoughtfully. "Actually, I don't really know because I haven't tested it yet. It may not even work at all."

"Yikes! It's eight thirty," Artemis said, glancing out the window at the giant sundial in the school courtyard. It was fifteen feet in diameter and could be seen from almost every window on this side of the school.

"Ye gods! We'd better get going," said Athena. Grabbing their stuff, the three girls hurried down the hall.

As they took the stairs down to the classroom levels, Athena noticed a gleaming white marble statue at the bottom of the main staircase. It was a girl, about five

121

feet tall, with long, flowing hair, wearing a chiton. "Is that statue new?"

"I've never seen it before," said Artemis.

"Me either," said Aphrodite.

Just then Persephone stepped from behind it. "Hi," she said, greeting them.

Athena jumped. "Oh! You scared me." Persephone's skin and white chiton were so pale that for a second, Athena had thought she might be another marble statue, coming to life.

"Sorry," said Persephone, turning to survey the statue. "I've been looking all over this thing, but there's no artist's signature on it anywhere. Who do you think made it?"

"Could it be Zeus's work?" suggested Aphrodite.

"I seriously doubt it," said Athena. Zeus was a ter-

122

rible artist, and this statue was so lifelike it seemed *real*. So real that it gave her the creeps.

"It looks familiar, though, don't you think?" said Artemis, cocking her head as she contemplated it. On either side of her, her dogs cocked their heads and stared at the statue too.

Before Athena could study the statue more carefully, the lyrebell pinged. The girls split up, saying quick good-byes as they dashed for their classes.

Athena grew a bit concerned when Medusa was absent from Hero-ology. "Something's up," she told Aphrodite. "I don't know what, but I have a bad feeling about that statue."

On the way down the hall to their second classes, Athena and Aphrodite saw that a crowd, which already included Persephone and Artemis, had gathered around the new statue. Everyone was speculating about who might have sculpted it.

As the two goddessgirls drew closer, unease swept over Athena. In the middle of its forehead, the statue's bangs were shaped like a question mark. She gasped. She must have been blind not to notice that before! "This statue looks just like . . . ," she began.

"Pandora!" Aphrodite finished for her.

"We just figured that out too," said Artemis.

Persephone frowned. "I have first period with Pandora, and she wasn't in class this morning."

"That's odd. Medusa wasn't in class either," said Athena. "I wonder if the two absences are connected?" Suddenly she heard a strange hissing sound. She turned to see Medusa standing directly behind her. She was wearing a hat.

"Oh, there you are," Athena said. "Have you seen Pandora?"

"No," Medusa replied, a little too innocently. "Wow, that statue looks just like her, doesn't it?" Only she didn't really sound surprised. There was something fakey in her voice. Or was it *snakey*?

"Why weren't you in Mr. Cyclops's class?" Aphrodite demanded.

Medusa smiled slyly. "I was doing my hair." She adjusted the large hat she was wearing.

Athena stared at it. "Is your hat . . . *wiggling*!?"

"Yep." With a dramatic flourish, Medusa whipped the hat off. Instead of hair, her head now writhed with hissing green snakes. The crowd of students recoiled in horror.

"Ye gods!" exclaimed Athena, jumping back.

"You took Athena's Snakeypoo, didn't you?" Artemis accused.

At the mention of the silly name, laughter rippled over the onlookers.

"It's not Snakeypoo. It's *Snarky*poo!" Athena corrected, feeling a little embarrassed.

"Looks like snakes to me," said Persephone, eyeing Medusa's hair.

"It's one of my inventions—a shampoo," Athena explained. "Anyway, I didn't know it would do"—she gestured toward the snakes—"that."

Shrugging, Medusa reached up to pet one of the reptiles. It coiled around her wrist, flicking its tongue, then uncoiled itself again. "Actually, I kind of like the power it gives me."

Aphrodite and Athena shot worried looks at

126

each other. "What power?" Aphrodite asked.

Medusa glanced Athena's way. "Did I mention that some of your goo dripped into my eyes during my shower this morning?"

"Serves you right," said Artemis.

Athena remained silent, thinking hard. What kind of power could Medusa mean? She glanced at the statue of Pandora and then back at Medusa. Suddenly something clicked. "Oh, no! This is all my fault! Snarkypoo was supposed to turn snarky words into stone. But because I misspelled the name as Snakeypoo, it turned hair into snakes. And it gave whoever used it the power to turn—"

"Pandora into stone?" Aphrodite guessed in a horrified voice.

Idly stroking one of her reptiles, Medusa sent

Athena a sly glance. "Now you know how it feels to have someone you care about mooched from you!"

"It isn't *her* fault Poseidon doesn't like you," gritted Aphrodite.

"Maybe he would if you were a little nicer," Persephone suggested helpfully.

"And less snakey," added Athena.

Medusa's snakes hissed, tongues flicking as they strained toward her. Athena backed away.

"Unfortunately, these snakes only give me the power to turn mortals to stone," Medusa said pointedly. "But I'm planning a little trip down to Triton after school today. What's the name of your mortal friend who lives in Triton City? I think I'll pay her a visit."

Athena gasped. "You leave my friends alone!"

"Anyone who's mortal, don't look into Medusa's

eyes!" Aphrodite warned the crowd. "She'll turn you to stone!"

The few mortals in the group ducked and ran for cover, hiding their eyes. But her warning came too late for Artemis's dogs. As Medusa whistled to them to get their attention, all three became encased in white stone.

"Turn them back, right this minute!" Artemis growled at Medusa. Aphrodite and Persephone held her back, worried the snakes might be poisonous.

"No, I don't think so," Medusa replied, studying her own glossy green fingernails.

While they were at a standoff, Athena spotted Poseidon standing by the nectar fountain. She pushed her way through the crowd and grabbed hold of his arm. "You have to help me stop her."

"Me?" he squeaked, pulling away. "Nuh-uh. I'm afraid of snakes." His pale turquoise cheeks turned pink, and he glanced around to see if anyone had overheard.

"Medusa won't hurt you. She likes you," Athena coaxed. "Besides, her powers only work on mortals, not godboys."

"Are you absolutely sure about that?"

"Of course—I invented Snarkypoo for mortals, after all. That's what the Invention Fair is all about," Athena assured him. "C'mon. Don't you want to be a hero?"

Poseidon sighed. "I guess." But he eyed Medusa's snakes warily.

"Good," Athena said quickly. Then she explained what she wanted him to do.

"All right," said Poseidon, still reluctant. "I just hope this works like you think it will."

A moment later he called out, "Oh, Meh-DOO-sah!"

Medusa's hair rattled and hissed as she turned to gaze out over the heads of the crowd to locate the speaker. Everyone ducked to avoid her eyes, even though most of them were godboys and goddessgirls, and therefore immune to her stare.

"Oh, hi, Poseidon," she cooed when she saw him.

"You look nice today," he fibbed, stopping a half dozen feet away from her.

"Thanks." Beaming, she coyly curled a snake around one finger.

"Only, um, there's something stuck between your teeth," he added. "Some green stuff."

"Really?" Medusa slapped a hand over her mouth, looking embarrassed. She pulled a tissue from the pocket of her chiton and rubbed it over her front teeth. "Gone?" she asked him, showing her teeth.

He shook his head. "No, it's still there."

"Here, I've got a mirror. See for yourself," said Athena. From her bag, she pulled the shield-shaped mirror she'd gotten at the Perseus Shield Market back on Earth and handed it to Medusa.

Medusa snatched the mirror away, lifted it . . . and gazed at her own reflection. Instantly she and her snakey hair turned to stone.

"She fell for it!" said Poseidon.

"Lucky for us, it really does work on mortals," Athena said, her eyes gleaming.

Aphrodite clapped both her hands together and laughed. "How brilliant! You made Medusa turn *herself* to stone!"

Around them everyone gaped at the new statue, whispering. Then slowly they started to cheer in relief.

Athena grinned at Poseidon. "Good job," she said, giving him a high five. Girls began to surround him, fawning and pushing Athena aside. "Aw, it was nothing," he said, more than willing to take credit.

Athena didn't mind. Those other girls were welcome to him. "Now I just need to figure out how to undo the spell on Pandora," she told her friends. "Watch her. I'll be back in a minute." With that she dashed off, taking the stairs two at a time to her dorm room.

Rummaging around on her desk, she found her Spell-ology textscroll and unfurled it. There were several thousand spells inside. Quickly scanning, she zipped past Anti–Bad Grade spells ("On any test I take today, let me earn a perfect A"), and Banishments ("Send these freckles from my skin, let them not appear again").

She skimmed past Enchantments that could bring forth lightning, love, or luck. Finally, near the end of the scroll, she found what she was looking for: Undo spells.

She ran her finger down the list. "Let's see. Unbaldy, Unclumsy, Undragon . . ." Finally she found it—an Unstatue spell.

Reading it over several times, she memorized it. Before the scroll had even snapped shut again, she was out the door and racing downstairs.

When she returned to the first floor, the other goddessgirls were still keeping watch over the statues. Kneeling, Artemis was petting her dogs' smooth white heads and looking sad.

Athena walked up to the statue of Pandora and placed a hand on her cold, white wrist. Standing on tiptoe she softly murmured into her ear, "Flesh and bone, return from stone!"

The statue of Pandora began to shake, then crumble. White dust filled the air as stone transformed back into skin, hair, chiton, and sandals.

"What happened?" asked Pandora, looking dazed. "Why is everyone staring at me?"

"You're back!" Aphrodite exclaimed. Giving her a fond hug that resulted in a big poof of white dust, she winked at Athena over her shoulder. "And already she's asking questions."

"What's going on? What's all this dust?" Pandora continued, as she combed bits of marble from her hair with her fingers.

"Medusa used one of my inventions to turn you to stone," explained Athena.

"Oh, really?" Pandora glared at the statue of Medusa. "Looks like it worked on her, too."

Quickly Athena reversed the spells on Artemis's dogs. They turned back into hounds, jumping and barking for joy as Artemis hugged them. Then they ran over to the statue of Medusa, growling as if to scold her.

Before Athena could approach Medusa and say the words that would change her back, Aphrodite grabbed her arm. "Wait!" she said.

"Yeah," said Pandora. "What's the rush?"

"I like her that way," agreed Persephone folding her arms. "Nice and quiet for a change."

Athena studied the marble statue of Medusa. Her face had frozen in a really weird position as she gazed at herself in the mirror. Her eyes looked a bit crossed, and her upper lip was curled to reveal her two front teeth.

Artemis snickered. "She looks like a cross-eyed beaver."

It was true, Athena realized, trying not to laugh. "But we can't really just leave her here like this," she said. "Can we?"

"Maybe just for a little while," suggested Pandora.

"Till tomorrow, after the Invention Fair," added Aphrodite.

"That should give the teachers enough time to decide what to do with her. After all, she can't be allowed to go running around turning mortals to stone whenever she feels like it," said Persephone.

Athena grinned, nodding slowly as she gazed at Medusa. "Excellent point. I mean, leaving her like this for a day or so couldn't hurt. In fact, it's a marble-ous idea!"

137

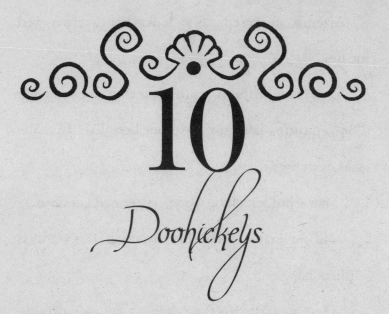

10

Doohickeys

AT THE INVENTION FAIR THE NEXT DAY,

everyone in the academy gathered in the gym to see

the inventions students had entered. Athena had only

just arrived when Aphrodite, Persephone, and Artemis

waved to her from a few tables away. She walked in

their direction, passing tables covered with fascinating

student entries. There were a few that seemed a little lame, however. The Sackrofice, for instance.

"Mortals are always giving immortals offerings of yucky stuff like lima beans. Stuff we don't want," the godboy who'd invented it told her when she paused at his table. "If you put the offerings in this sack, they'll disappear."

"Interesting," said Athena. "No one from Earth has offered me anything yet, yucky or otherwise, but I'll keep your invention in mind."

Some of the other inventions were just for fun. Like the Lucky-in-Love Lip Balm that made everyone fall in love with the wearer. That was Aphrodite's idea.

"Let me put some on you," she suggested when Athena reached her.

"Not me!" said Athena, horrified. "Try it on Artemis."

"No way!" said Artemis. She laughed good-naturedly as she backed away. "Try Persephone."

"I already did." Aphrodite pointed her out.

Sure enough, a pink-lipped Persephone stood nearby. She was surrounded by three godboys, all competing to see who could fawn over her the most.

"Could I fetch you a flagon of nectar?" one asked.

"Or some ambrosia?" suggested another.

"Not that you need either to be beautiful," said a third. "Your skin is as pale as the finest white marble from the quarry at Thassos."

Looking a bit flushed, Persephone caught Athena's eye. "I sure hope this stuff wears off soon," she said.

"Wow! Did you see Poseidon's invention?" Pandora asked, rushing up to them.

Athena clutched the box of inventions she'd brought to show. "Not yet." Glancing beyond Pandora and the rows and rows of tables, she saw that a crowd had gathered across the room. Poseidon stood in the middle of it.

"Hey, what's this?" asked Pandora, spying Aphrodite's lip balm. Before anyone could explain or stop her, Pandora had glossed her lips with it. Instantly Persephone's admirers transferred their attention to her.

"Phew," said Persephone, grabbing the chance to escape. She tugged at Athena and Artemis. "Let's go check out Poseidon's invention."

"Wait up, I'm coming too," said Aphrodite. "Watch my booth, Pandora?"

"Sure," said Pandora. She didn't seem to mind

when the godboys trailed after her. Instead she happily launched a barrage of questions at her captive audience. "So, I've always wondered—what do godboys talk about when goddessgirls aren't around? And why . . ."

As the four goddessgirls walked toward Poseidon, Athena could hear him proudly explaining how his invention worked. "See, you whoosh through the sea monster chute and then zoom out of its mouth into this big splash pool at the bottom of the slide," he was saying.

When the crowd shifted enough, Athena finally got a good look at his invention. It was a model of a magnificent water park he was planning to build on Earth! There were gracefully curving slides made of polished marble, mermaids and mermen, sea monsters, fountains, and pools of turquoise water topped with lily pads. A sign in front read POSEIDON WATER WAVES.

Wow was right, thought Athena. Poseidon was a shoo-in to win.

"What do you think of my park?" Poseidon asked when he saw her. "Think I'll win?"

"It looks like fun," Athena told him sincerely. Like a place even she'd like to go sometime. But of course it was for mortals only. She'd have to tell Pallas about it, though. "And you've got a great shot at the grand prize for sure."

Poseidon beamed. "Thanks. Are those your inventions?" he asked, glancing curiously at the box Athena was holding.

She shrugged. Her inventions paled in comparison. None were as good as a water park. She started to tell Poseidon that but was interrupted.

"Hear ye, hear ye!" bellowed Principal Zeus. Holding

a scroll, he climbed a set of stairs to stand on a raised stage in the middle of the gym.

"Gather around, godboys and goddessgirls of Mount Olympus Academy," he thundered. "A distinguished panel of Earth mortals visited our gym this very morning to judge all the inventions in this year's fair. They've just now sent a scroll to my office announcing the winner."

"Wait!" Aphrodite yelled, waving her hand to stop him. "Athena hasn't shown her inventions yet."

Athena grabbed her arm, shushing her. "I'm not going to enter."

"But you have to," Persephone chimed in. "You've worked hard on your inventions ever since you got here!"

"Do you really think a rake or a ship could beat a water park?" said Athena.

"Your ship's cool," said Artemis. "Come on. Try."

Aphrodite nodded encouragingly.

"No, it's too late," said Athena, managing to smile through her disappointment. "I'll just try again next year."

"And the winner is—" Zeus grinned in delight as he unrolled the scroll he held. His piercing blue eyes searched the crowd of students until they met Athena's. "The winner is my brainiest, most favorite daughter in the whole wide universe—Theeny!"

Athena gasped in astonishment. "But I couldn't have won. I didn't even enter," she murmured, just loud enough for her friends to hear.

"Maybe the mortals liked the inventions you brainstormed on Monday," suggested Artemis.

"The ones that beaned them on the head?" Athena scoffed. She was still embarrassed by what had happened the other day in the courtyard with Zeus.

"Anyway, you won!" said Aphrodite.

"Come up here and get your trophy, Theeny!" Zeus boomed. Even though she suspected there'd been some mistake, Athena couldn't help feeling thrilled by the pride in his voice.

"You heard him," said Persephone.

"Yeah, go on up there," added Artemis.

The three goddessgirls pushed Athena forward. When she got close enough, Zeus lifted her onstage to stand next to him. She tried not to flinch at the sizzle of electricity that shot down her arms.

"Theeny! Girl, you've done me and the academy proud!" his voice rumbled. "Earth is tickled pink with your invention."

"They liked the ship?" Athena guessed. "Or was it the rake?"

"No and no. I mean they liked those okay, of course. But what really wowed them were these little round doohickeys that go in salads." He held up a little black oval ball between his thumb and forefinger.

"They liked my olives?" Athena asked in surprise.

"Not liked. They *loved* 'em. And they're not only eating them, they're squeezing oil out of the little suckers to burn in their lamps and to heat their homes. They're even making perfume and medicine out of 'em. One group are such fans that they want to rename their town 'Athens' in your honor."

"Ye gods," said Athena, stunned.

"Yep, you and your olives are a sensation down there on Earth! Good job, Theeny!" With that, Zeus tossed the olive he held high in the air, letting it plop back in his mouth. He chomped it loudly for a moment, then spit out its pit.

Ptooey! The pit soared upward in an arc, before dropping into the crowd. Students dodged this way and that, trying not to let it hit them.

"My only objection is the pits," mused Zeus. "See if you can do something about those, Theeny girl."

"O-okay," said Athena. She glanced over at Poseidon, who looked shocked that he'd lost to an olive. Angling her head to indicate him, she told Zeus, "I'm glad they liked the olives, but did they see Poseidon's water park? It's pretty amazing."

"Thunderation! That reminds me." Zeus turned to the crowd again. "I have another announcement to make," he boomed. "Second place goes to Poseidon Water Waves! Come on up, Posey boy!"

Poseidon's face lit up, and he hurried to join them onstage.

Suddenly Zeus got a funny look on his face. He frowned and cocked his head, as if he were listening to a voice only he could hear. "Take out the trash? You're reminding me now, in the middle of an awards ceremony?" he groused. As he listened a little more, his frown faded. "Oh, yeah, I almost forgot that."

He turned his attention back to Athena. "Your mom just reminded me to give you this." He dragged a huge trophy forward to show her. "It's from both of us." It was the same trophy she'd seen him working on that first day she'd visited his office, and it was just as ugly as she remembered.

"Thanks, I love it," she said honestly. No matter how ugly it was, it was a gift from her parents—and she would cherish it.

"Your mom sends her congratulations too, obviously."

"Do you think I could talk to her myself one of these days?" Athena suggested bravely.

"Sure! I'll have to translate because she's a fly and all, but we'll work it out."

Athena's heart soared. "Deal. Thanks, Princi—Dad." Even if he wasn't exactly what she'd expected in the beginning, she was starting to feel glad Principal Zeus was her father.

Just then Poseidon joined them on the stage.

"Now you two winners get to choose your prizes," Zeus told them, proudly placing a hand on each of their shoulders.

Before Athena could speak, Poseidon whipped out a list he'd prepared and began reading. "First off, I'd like mortals to name a chewing gum after my trident, so no one will ever call it a pitchfork again," he told Zeus. "And I'd like to be Earth's official water park designer. And I'd like lots of statues of me to be placed in fountains everywhere." He tucked the list back into his pocket.

"It shall be done," proclaimed Zeus, handing him a small gold trophy. Beaming, Poseidon left the stage, waving his trophy high in triumph. The crowd cheered wildly. Especially the girls.

Then Zeus turned to Athena. "And you? What prize would you like?"

Athena already knew what she wanted most. "I was wondering if . . ." She crossed her fingers for luck behind her back before continuing. "I was wondering— could my friend Pallas from Earth come visit?" she finished, the words tumbling out.

"A mortal?" Zeus's black eyebrows lifted doubtfully. "Is she gifted in some way?"

"Sort of. She's a good friend—a gift to me. It's just a visit. Pleeease?" Athena pleaded, hoping as hard as she could.

After a long minute and intense discussion with the fly in his head, Zeus said, "Okay, why not?"

Muscles bulged in his arm as he pointed a finger

toward an empty spot in the center of the stage. "In the name of Zeus, let it be done!"

Zap! A bolt of lightning shot from his fingertips. When the smoke cleared, Pallas stood there on the stage between them.

Her dark, wavy hair was sticking out in all directions, and she was wearing her pajamas. Not only had Zeus transported her to Mount Olympus—it looked like he had gotten her out of bed!

Yawning, Pallas glanced around as if she thought she must be dreaming.

"Ye gods! I didn't mean now," Athena told Zeus. "She's not even dressed."

Pallas scratched her elbow, then stretched, yawning again.

"Should I send her back?" Zeus asked, looking confused.

"No!" Athena rolled her eyes. Honestly, parents just didn't get it sometimes.

"Sorry about the pj's, Pal," Athena told her friend.

"Am I really on Mount Olympus?" Pallas asked, beginning to look more excited. And more awake. She reached out and touched Athena's arm. "Is that really you, Athena, or am I dreaming?"

Athena grinned, squeezing her hand. "It's me, and yes, this is really Mount Olympus. If Zeus sends a message to your parents, can you stay for the weekend?"

"Are you serious? Yes!" shouted Pallas. She and Athena hugged and began jumping around the stage together in a little circle.

"Thanks, Dad," Athena told Zeus. She was so happy,

she hugged him, too, but quickly let go when she got zapped.

Zeus grinned, noisily chomping another olive. "Anything for my Theeny." Giving her a huge smile and grabbing a jar of olives under one muscle-bound arm, he leaped off the stage and headed back in the direction of his office.

"I wonder what I should do with this," Athena said, looking at the huge statue he'd left her with. She still couldn't figure out what kind of bird it was supposed to be.

"I'll take care of it," Aphrodite called from where she was standing with the other goddessgirls in front of the stage. Summoning the four nearest godboys she saw, she smiled at them and asked, "Would you mind taking this to the trophy case? I'd really appreciate it."

They practically fell over themselves rushing onstage to impress the prettiest goddessgirl in school, then huffed and puffed Athena's trophy off through the gym toward the trophy room.

"Thanks, Aphrodite," said Athena.

"Aphrodite?" Pallas echoed, gazing at her in awe.

"Come meet my new goddessgirl friends," Athena said, pulling her old pal down to the gym floor to meet the others. "Hey, everyone, this is Pallas, my friend from Earth."

As the girls introduced themselves, Pandora ran up. "Guess what?" she said after she'd been introduced too. "I made the flag team, and you all made the GG Squad! The list was just posted on the bulletin board!"

"Woo-hoo!" shouted Artemis.

"*Wooooo,*" howled her dogs.

"Let's go celebrate!" said Persephone.

"What about Medusa?" asked Athena as they started out of the gym. She didn't miss her one bit, but she wasn't sure if they should just leave her as she was.

Aphrodite grinned. "Later."

"Yeah, she's not going anywhere," added Artemis.

"Why spoil the celebration?" said Pandora.

Athena smiled. "Well, then, let's go!"

"Who's Medusa?" asked Pallas as they started to walk again. She was looking a little dizzy and overwhelmed. "I've never heard of a goddess with that name."

"C'mon. We'll fill you in," said Athena, linking arms with her. "It's been a busy week. I can hardly wait to tell you everything!"

"Wow! I can't believe I get to hang around with goddesses for a whole weekend! And—" Suddenly Pallas stopped in her tracks. "Oh. My. Godness!" she said in a faint voice. She lifted a shaking finger toward the Water Waves exhibit they were passing. "Is th-that— Poseidon?"

Seeing her interest, Poseidon shot her a gleaming smile and winked.

Pallas blushed.

"Another one bites the dust," murmured Artemis.

Athena hid a smile. "I'll introduce him to you later, if you'd like," she said. "But maybe you'd better change your clothes first."

"Ye gods!" Pallas exclaimed, her face turning red. "I forgot I was still wearing pj's!"

"Don't worry," said Aphrodite. "I've got something that would look great on you."

As the girls headed off for the dorm, Athena thought

how happy she was to be with her old friend Pallas and her new friends, Aphrodite, Persephone, Artemis, and Pandora. When it came right down to it, the students at MOA weren't so very different from those on Earth. While most were nice, Medusa and her sisters were just like some of the queen bees at her old school.

"The academy is so beautiful," said Pallas, gaping at the paintings and statues when they entered the school building.

"It is, isn't it?" said Athena, hearing the pride in her own voice.

Pallas leaned close, so only Athena would hear. "So you're happy here? You fit in?"

"Yeah," Athena assured her. "I am. I do."

It was true, she realized. She did fit in here. Amid girls with snake hair and boys who made squishing sounds when they walked, she was practically normal! And though the past week had been difficult, having good friends had made things easier, and her studies interested her way more than those at Triton Junior High ever had. Not that her problems were over, of course. She'd need her new friends to help guide her in her schoolwork and in the rules of being a goddess-girl. But she was looking forward to the challenges ahead. And to getting to know Zeus and her mom better too.

"Yeah, I have a feeling I'm going to be very happy at Mount Olympus Academy," said Athena. Smiling, she tugged Pallas toward the stairs. "C'mon. I can hardly wait to show you around!"

READ ON FOR THE NEXT ADVENTURE

WITH THE

Goddess Girls

PERSEPHONE
THE PHONY

A LYREBELL PINGED, SIGNALING THE END OF another Monday at Mount Olympus Academy. Persephone crammed the textscroll she'd been reading into her scrollbag and got up to leave the library. As she joined the throng of godboys and goddessgirls streaming into the hallway, a herald appeared on the balcony above them. "The twenty-third day of the school year is now at an end," he announced in a loud, important voice. Then he struck his lyrebell again with a little hammer.

A brown-haired goddessgirl carrying so many

scrolls she could barely see over the top of them fell into step beside Persephone. "Ye gods. That means one hundred seventeen days to go!"

"Hi, Athena." Persephone pointed to the pile of scrolls. "Some light reading?" she joked.

"Research," said Athena. She was the brainiest of Persephone's friends, and also the youngest, though they were all in the same grade.

The two goddessgirls continued past a golden fountain. Persephone's eyes flickered over a painting on the wall beyond it, showing Helios, the sun god, mounting to the sky in his horse-drawn carriage. The academy was filled with paintings celebrating the exploits of the gods and goddesses. They were so inspiring!

"Hey, you guys, wait up!" called a goddessgirl in a pale blue chiton—the flowing gown that was all the rage among goddesses and mortal Greek women right now. Aphrodite, the most *gorgeous* of Persephone's friends, raced toward the two girls across gleaming marble tiles. Her long golden hair, held in place by seashell clips, streamed behind her as she dodged past a godboy who was part goat. He bleated, but when he saw who it was, he stared after her with an admiring, doe-eyed look.

"I'm going to the Immortal Marketplace this afternoon," Aphrodite said breathlessly. "Artemis was supposed to go with me, but she's got archery practice. Want to come?"

Athena sagged under her load of scrolls. "I don't know," she said. "I've got so much work to do."

"It can wait," said Aphrodite. "Don't you want to go shopping?"

"Well," said Athena, "I *could* use some new knitting supplies." Athena was always knitting something. Her last project was a striped woolen cap. She'd made it for Mr. Cyclops, the Hero-ology teacher, to cover his bald head.

"You'll come too, right, Persephone?" Aphrodite asked.

Persephone hesitated. She didn't really want to go to the mall, but she was afraid of hurting Aphrodite's feelings. Too bad she didn't have a good excuse like Artemis. But except for cheering with the Goddess Squad, Persephone wasn't much into sports. "I . . . uh . . . I'd *love* to go," she said at last. Her mom would have been proud. She was always telling Persephone to be polite and "go along to get along."

Goddess Girls

✳ **READ ABOUT ALL
YOUR FAVORITE GODDESSES!**

#1 ATHENA THE BRAIN

#2 PERSEPHONE
THE PHONY

#3 APHRODITE
THE BEAUTY

#4 ARTEMIS THE BRAVE

From Aladdin

PUBLISHED BY SIMON & SCHUSTER